What a Day!

also by Almut and Robert Gernhardt

ONE MORE MAKES FOUR

What a Day!

Pictures by Almut Gernhardt
with verses by Robert Gernhardt
translated from the German by
Kathrine Talbot

Jonathan Cape
Thirty Bedford Square London

If in summer we've money and time to spare,
we leave the city and its stale air,
the lack of space, the crowds and cars
to enjoy the sun, the moon and stars.
But with a holiday in mind
we don't want to leave our pets behind.
Where we've gone Min's always been;
she's with us now but can't be seen.
If you can't guess where she can be,
just carry on and you will see.

A box or basket when it's closed
is full of promise. No one knows

what is inside. Now we see more,
someone is in there, I am sure.

It's animal. But whether friend or foe
it is too early yet to know.

At first they both felt rather shy,

but they drew closer by and by.

At such a time it helps to be
ready with perfect courtesy

to get acquainted. This makes them feel
that their friendship is now real.

"My name is Tom. What do they call you?"
"I am called Min, but listen, do,
I want to ask you straight away,

can I start hunting here today?"

"Hunting? Whatever will you catch?"
"Just anything that I can snatch."
"Why – are you hungry?
Wait for your next dish."
"That's not the same. You see, I wish
to quench my thirst to hunt, my passion."
"But have you ever hunted in this fashion?"

"Never before, but will not fail
to make the animal kingdom quail!
Oh lead me where the zebra graze
and with my claws I'll them amaze.
Show me the herds of antelope
to give my hunting prowess scope.
Where are you, hordes of buffalo?
Ferocious speed to you I'll show!"
"Of buffalo? What can you mean?
We're not in Africa where they are seen!
Our wildlife here is rather small,
the hedgehog largest of them all."
"The hedgehog?"
"Yes, look here comes one."

"Take care, my laddie, or you're gone,
for hedgehog is my favourite grub!

Watch now, as I just . . .

... rip him up ...
Or rather I don't want to plague

so small an animal. Now don't be vague,
please recommend some other prey."

"Be sensible, desist today,
the country's lovely on the whole,
let's first go for a nice long stroll,
and I'll explain as we go on
the things that grow here. Come along!
Don't be afraid, I'll lead the way."
And Tom starts off without delay.

Min follows after with dislike,
she wants to hunt and not to hike.

"Fine wine is made from this ripe fruit,"
says Tom, but Min cares not a hoot.

"These trees are cypresses," adds Tom.
Min yawns, as fed up as they come.

"I hope these figs you recognise!"
But Min has firmly closed her eyes.

"And yonder stands an olive grove."
Min is so bored that she won't move.

"And look at those delightful herbs!"
Now Min uses some strong words
and hisses, "Damn your greenery,
and blast your boring scenery.
I'm off."
"What did you say?"
"I'm off to hunt, so long, good day!
Will you come with me?"
"No, not I."
"All right, I'll see you by and by.
But one thing I will promise straight:
I shall be back with you at eight
and bring along a mammoth prey!"
"You'll never do it!" – "Speed the day!"

 And while Tom gives a Cheshire grin,
away to hunt goes gallant Min.

The clock strikes two. The sun is hot.
Everyone sleeps, but Min does not.

"Who says this is no hunting region?
Look just ahead, my prey is legion!
I see a herd of grandiose scale."
Min crouches low and waves her tail:
"Those pigs are grazing quite phlegmatic."
She flings herself on them, ecstatic.

"These pigs have neither legs nor head!"
If Min could blush her face would now be red,

and she takes off with utmost haste
to find a prey more to her taste.

The goldfinch sways upon his bough,
the stalker thinks, "I have you now!"

Not every leap reaches its aim:
the prickly thorns are much to blame

for this great hunter's nasty fall.
But Min, not being hurt at all,

makes off towards a shady stable,
thinking that she might well be able

to combine coolness with pursuit,
which shows that she is quite astute.
A stable makes her think of mice:
she might well catch one in a trice.
But one does have to lie in wait
for mice, which could well make her late
for eight o'clock. She sits and quivers,
a rustle sends her into shivers.

Is there a mouse beneath this cask?
Min concentrates upon her task.
Now is the moment! Tally-ho!

The mouse says nothing down below.

The clock strikes seven. Not a hope
that in one hour she could cope
and so act upon her solemn oath.
"Oh," she sighs sadly, "I am loth
to return now. Will no one lend a hand?"
"But yes!"
"Who's there? I do not understand!"
A louder voice replies, "I guess,

my friend, that you are in a mess."

"Who is it?" Min asks, quite confused.
"Me," says the stranger, much amused.
"I've followed you for a long while.
I must confess, I like your style.
And since you are – hm – quite my type,
and I consider Tom just ripe
for a surprise, and I like you
being both nice and clumsy too,
my splendid scheme you now shall hear."
The rest is whispered in Min's ear.

It must give her a proper thrill,
for Min says, "That just fills the bill.
Thank you for helping me in need,"
and hurries off to do the deed.

The time has come. The clock strikes eight,
neither of our friends is late.
We see the moon, a silver ball,
a pair of cats upon the wall.
One of the two looks quite amazed,
the other pleased, but rather dazed.

Tom says, "Whatever have we here?"
Which makes Min grin from ear to ear.
"It isn't very much today,
just part of a much larger prey
which I have left in a safe spot."
"Whatever monster have you got?"
"Well, that is rather hard to say,
I want to ask you anyway.
It was a pretty strange affair,

for ostrich legs it had a pair,

but its enormous body bore
spots like a jaguar. What's more

a swanlike neck arose from there
to hold a head which, as it were,
reminds me of a buffalo."

"Stop, stop! How can you scare me so?

And you have killed that fearful beast?"
"Who else? It seemed to me the least
that I could do. I saw it trot, its head held high
towards the waterhole near by
and thought at once: I want that one!
A mighty paw-stroke and 'twas done.
I don't believe it suffered greatly.
Let's dine! I haven't eaten lately."
"Me too?" asks Tom in eager haste –

They race to eat, no time to waste.

The meal is done. The clock strikes nine.
Tom, feeling sleepy and just fine
curls up and in a thoughtful way
says, "Quite amazing! What a day!"
And goes to sleep and does not hear
when someone drawing softly near,
black as the devil, eyes all bright,

says, "Sister, was my plan all right?"
"Quite splendid, for the animal was just
where you had told me, and I trust
I nabbed it without being seen."
"And Tom?"
"He was quite taken in."
"Magnificent! Do I get some?"
"The rest is yours. I hoped you'd come."
"Oh, much obliged," says her black friend,

and soon the meal is at an end.

Darkness has fallen. But indoors
the lamps go on, and no one snores;
not only can one see much light
but hear the people, loud and bright,
where some excited voices call,
"I never moved the thing at all!
I put it here upon the sill . . ."
"I saw it there, it was there still."
And someone says, "What is the matter?"
And someone else, "Here is the platter
the leg of lamb was laid upon.
Have you not see it? It has gone."
And someone calls, "No, no, not me!"
A voice laments, "Where can it be?"
While someone thinks, "How very queer
that neither of the cats is here.
What can the darlings be about,
not to come home but to stay out?
Nor condescend, so it would seem,
to lap their evening bowl of cream?"

But Tom sleeps deeply and serene,
quite undisturbed, and in between
the two the little black friend lies,
nestling near Min, who's closed her eyes,
and thinks and ponders, "What a day!
I'm ready for tomorrow's fray."

And then she too goes to sleep.

Published in Great Britain 1980
First published in Germany 1978 under the title
Was für ein Tag
© Insel Verlag Frankfurt am Main 1978

Translation © 1980 by Jonathan Cape Ltd
Jonathan Cape Ltd, 30 Bedford Square, London WC1

British Library Cataloguing in Publication Data

Gernhardt, Robert
What a day!
I. Title   II. Gernhardt, Almut
833'.9'1J   PZ7.G311/

ISBN 0 224 01844 2

Printed in Germany